BIG AND LITTLE

BIG AND LITTLE

by RUTH KRAUSS

illustrated by MARY SZILAGYI

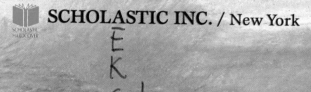

SCHOLASTIC INC. / New York

SCHOLASTIC HARDCOVER is a trademark of Scholastic Inc.
Art direction/design by Diana Hrisinko

Library of Congress Cataloging-in-Publication Data
Krauss, Ruth.
Big and little.
Summary: Brief text and illustrations describe some
of the little things that big things love.
[1. Size—Fiction. 2. Love—Fiction] I. Szilagyi, Mary,
ill. II. Title.
PZ7.K875Bg 1987   [E]   86-33859
ISBN 0-590-41707-X

12 11 10 9 8 7 6 5 4 3 2 1   7 8 9/8 0 1 2/9

Printed in the U.S.A.   23

FIRST SCHOLASTIC PRINTING, OCTOBER 1987

To Anne

—M.S.

big forests

love
little trees

big fields

love
little flowers

big monkeys
love
little monkeyshines

and I love you

big seas

love
little shells

big stories
love
little words to fly around in

big skies
love
little skyscrapers

and I love you

big dark streets

love
little streetlamps

big sorrows

love
little tears

big kings
love
a little butter on their bread

and I love you

deand